"WHOEVER HEARD OF A PURPLE HAPPY TREE?"

Enjoy!
Joyce Timberlake
Angelia Carol Wright

Joyce Timberlake

ISBN: 978-1-63945-154-8 (Paperback)
        978-1-63945-155-5 (Ebook)

The views expressed in this book are solely those of the author and do not necessarily reflect the views of the publisher, and the publisher hereby disclaims any responsibility for them.

Writers' Branding
1800-608-6550
www.writersbranding.com
orders@writersbranding.com

"Whoever Heard of a Purple Happy Tree."

The Four Sisters Books: WEBSITES:

Joyce Timberlake
joyce-timberlake.pixels.com

Angelcia Carol Wright
angelcia-wright.pixels.com

Barbara Hall Adkins
Barbarahall-adkins.pixels.com

Sandra Moore
In memory of Sandra Hall Moore

Everybody should have a happy tree by Joy!

"...There is a balance between innocent playfulness and the conflicts between creatures with plenty of action to please readers of all ages. The story takes surprising twists and turns. Educators, parents and children will find themselves spellbound by the story and its captivating art."

- US Review of Books

This book is dedicated to my children:
Karen, Sharon, Mike & Angie
In Memory of Karen Marie Friend

The Happy Tree is a mischievous, lovable little creature who is an outcast from his forest home because he accidentally started a fire with a "magic glass on a stick" (magnifying glass). In the process of trying to save the youngest Joy Baby, Angie, **The Happy Tree** uses the leaves on his top knot to smother the fire. But something terrible happened! His leaves changed from green to purple! When this happened, he became a social outcast with the tree town elders. The Happy Tree is the Joy Babies' constant companion. You are sure to be spellbound by his colorful antics and playful tricks. The Happy Tree is going to be a special legend! Plant a TREE and you will SEE! YOU will be HAPPY too! I LOVE TREES AND I LOVE ME! Did you ever hear of the HAPPY TREE? I'm the cutest thing you'll ever see! **I AM the HAPPY TREE!** The National Theme**: "Everybody Should Have a Happy Tree by Joy!"**

"HAVE YOU EVER HEARD OF THE HAPPY TREE?"

Have you ever heard of the Happy Tree?

He's the cutest thing you'll ever see, The Happy Tree.

If you want to see the Happy Tree, just dream along with me.

Close your eyes and off we'll go to the land of Joy

that we all know.

Ho, Ho, I'm as Happy as can be, I'm so jolly, I am happy, I am me

Now, think about that little tree.

So, watch through the rain for the Happy Tree

Here comes the sunshine now what do you see, ho, ho, he, hee

It's the Happy Tree!

We'll fly over the rainbow to the other side, 'til we see the

rainforest below, that old rainforest is scary to see.

From his dancing roots to his leaves so green

he's the cutest thing you've ever seen,

Oh, it makes you want to sing this song so loud

It will ring through the treetops and down to the sea

Are you glad you came with me

I'm so jolly, I am free, I'm so happy, I am me.

Now think about that little tree

Ho, Ho, Hee, Hee

TABLE OF CONTENTS

"Whoever Heard of a Purple Happy Tree?"

BY Joyce Timberlake

CHAPTER 1

The Morning Glory Patch

Once upon a time, there were four beautiful little babies. They lived in the Kingdom of Joy. Joyland is an enchanting forest full of trees that are alive! These babies are Joy Babies. They are delicate and pastel colored. They have wings so they could flit and flutter about in the forest spreading love and happiness everywhere they flew. Their tiny feet shimmer in satin sandals which glow in the dark as they flutter about and their bodies are clothed in yards and yards of sparkles. Their heads are adorned with lovely, fresh flowers, picked daily to accent their sparkles. The babies live in a morning glory patch next to Timber Lake. They are near a mysterious castle where the mean Rainforest Trees live in Joyland.

Early each morning they awake and watch the sun rise high over the East while rubbing the sleep out of their eyes. They are fascinated by all the bright colors. The colors promise them their day would be filled with excitement, adventure and best of all, fun! The morning glories waited anxiously as the dew fell on their tiny petals and opened them. Stretching from a good night's sleep, they excitedly approached the day.

The morning glories beg to be a part of the Joy Babies' hair ornaments. They love to play and want to be a part of the day's excitement, because every day the Joy Babies do so many fun things! "Pick me! Pick me," they beg, but only a few will be selected. One day they discovered someone new in their playground. It was a tree unlike any other tree in Joyland. He was smaller than the rest and looked like he wanted to join in the fun.

3

When they asked who he was, he sadly replied, "I don't have a name." When Angie Baby asked where he lived, he replied, "I don't know, I think I'm lost!" Angie Baby winked. It was a signal to her friends and they knew what she meant. The little tree was in the dark, of course. He looked surprised when the four Joy Babies flew to his nest of unkempt locks and perched playfully.

Ruffles the Squirrel grabbed the little tree's hand as the little quacklings started doing somersaults over one another. The little tree smiled broadly. It had been a long time since he laughed and it felt good! When one of the quacklings misjudged a jump and fell into the brook, the little tree wiggled his trunk and giggled with glee! He giggled so hard, it made everyone else laugh. "I know, I know! We'll give you a name!" said Mikie, the only boy Joy Baby. Karen and Sharon, the two oldest girl Joy Babies chimed in, as if they all knew what each other were thinking. They all shouted at the same time, "We will call you Happy! **The Happy Tree!**"

And Happy it was. Everyday all the wood creatures meet Happy Tree and race to Timber Lake where Lara LaQuack and her little Quacklings dwell. Before long, the Joy Babies fly in with their ornaments of freshly picked flowers, still sprinkled with the morning dew. They are carefully arranged in their long flowering golden locks. The Joy Babies weave flowers into their hair each morning without fail because the freshness of the flowers light their sparkles. At night, when the flowers lose their freshness and droop, their sparkles dim, and the Joy Babies fall asleep in the morning dew patch.

One day the Joy Babies prepared to meet their new-found friend down by Timber Lake. As they flitted and fluttered about, they became distraught. Someone had trampled the grass down by the water! The grass was full of trash! "Maybe someone had a picnic!" shouted Sharon Baby. "Let's go see!" The forest was always so clean and beautiful that the little bit of trash marred the beauty of their playground by Timber Lake.

"No! No! No! This is no way to start a new day!" cried Angie Baby, the littlest girl Joy Baby. "We'll just have to clean it up!" They flew to get some help from the wood creatures because they were too small to pick up the larger pieces of trash. "Hurry, Hurry!" they exclaimed, as the wood creatures, rubbing their eyes of sleep, scampered over the hill and down to the brook. "We want to play today, so we will have to hurry and clean up this mess!"

Everyone picked up the small pieces and discarded them in the old scooped out stump that Groundy Groundhog had rolled down to them to put the trash in. "I don't believe this," he grumbled roughly. "I wanted to play, not work!" The quacklings and the woodcreatures were very upset. "I want to play too, I don't like work, this is no fun!" cried Sandy the squirrel. As they were scooping trash into the stump, someone asked, "Where is the Happy Tree?" They needed some help, and Happy was bigger than the rest of them. "Angie!" exclaimed Karen, "Go and find Happy! I want to see if he knows what I just found!" "What did you find?" Angie asked. "Find The Happy Tree and maybe he will know what this is. Then we will all know!" said Karen.

9

CHAPTER 2
The Fire

Suddenly, the Happy Tree jumped over a log and yelled, "What's up?" At the same time he yelled he was trying to clear the log but his roots clicked together causing him to fall flat on his face. As he grinned and looked up, he came face to face with Karen Baby. "You are always clowning around Happy, see what we found? What do you think this is?" Karen asked as she grinned at the funny looking little tree. "A magic glass! Look! It's on a stick!" Happy said gleefully.

Karen picked up the magnifying glass carefully. "It's broken," The Happy Tree said. "Don't cut yourself," said the little tree. "Let's see if it works!" She put the magnifying glass close to a colorful butterfly sitting on a beautiful flower. Everyone gathered around to see how the magic glass worked. Karen moved the object back and forth over the butterfly so the others could see how much bigger it made the wings and the flower petals look.

"Look how big that butterfly is!" said the Doofless goose in an excited voice. "It looks like a monster!" said Ruffles the Squirrel. But while all the others were watching the beautiful wings of the butterfly move slowly up and down, Angie Baby had made her own discovery. "Look at all the pretty colors!" she cried. She pointed her small finger at the ground close to the magnifying glass. All the others turned to see what she was talking about. The sun shining through the curved glass made a small rainbow of colors that danced on the ground as Karen moved it. When the magic glass was turned a certain way, the colors would burst into sunbeams. An artist's palette emerged with every shade of color imaginable!

Happy clapped his hands together. "Oh, how beautiful!" he exclaimed. But as all the creatures watched the colors sparkling so playfully through the magnifying glass, they failed to recognize the danger of the warmth of the sun's rays. With everyone's attention on the dancing lights, no one noticed what was happening to the dry leaves on the ground as the beam of light glowed upon them. The sun shining through the glass made the sun's rays get very hot, and the heat on the leaves start to smoke. Suddenly, a spark of fire sprang up among the dried leaves, frightening everyone. Karen dropped the magnifying glass and ran away, with the little wood creatures close behind.

13

"Oh nooooo!" everyone exclaimed, for they knew the dangers of fire. Horrified, they watched as the fire spread quickly along the ground. Lara LaQuack grabbed her Quackling and waddled safely to the cool water as Shawn Swan stood frozen in fear. As if on cue, when they saw the Quacklings leap into the safety of their mother's arms, they also turned and fled, some to the water and others off through the terrified trees.

Wally B. Walnut grabbed his small son, Twig, while Wilma Willow sheltered the Joy Babies from the ravishing effects of the blaze. The elders of Joyland hurriedly ran towards the fire.

Mayor Roots was furious! How dare a perfect stranger enter his town and cause such a mess! He looked the situation over, saw the leftover bits of trash and garbage, along with the quickly spreading fire, and decided it must have been the stranger's fault.

15

Meanwhile, Angie Baby was missing! Wilma Willow counted the Joy Babies and discovered the littlest Joy Baby was lost amongst all the shuffle and confusion. "Oh, we must find her," her panicky brother and sisters exclaimed! They were worried about the safety of their sister. Sassy Sassafras and Oadie Oak were carrying buckets filled with water to the dangerous heat. Everyone joined in fighting the forest fire. Mayor Roots wrung his hands in sorrow. "Ohhhh, ohhhh," he cried. "We must find her!"

No one ever thought of Happy. Since he was a stranger to the town, not many trees even knew about him. The few trees that saw him did not realize that he was more than just a visitor. He had stayed with the wood creatures and the Joy Babies. Since he had arrived in Joyland, he had never met a lot of the others who lived there. The Great Bald Eagle, Enoch, watched closely as the little tree and the Joy Baby ran from the forest. He decided he had better follow them before anything else happened.

CHAPTER 3

The Rescue

What everyone didn't know was that Angie Baby had been hurt! She had run in the same direction as Happy when the fire started and had tripped over the root of an old rotten tree! Stunned, she watched as Happy raced ahead. She realized she was in grave danger. The fire was spreading rapidly along the ground and had almost caught up with her. Sobbing, she buried her face in the ground. The smoke hung heavy in the air. Angie had injured her wings in the fall and didn't have the strength to fly away from the dangerous flames.

18

The Happy Tree, in all the excitement, had been too scared to look back and did not even realize that Angie Baby had followed him. Suddenly, he remembered why he had been lost when he came to the strange forest. "This is what happened before!" he thought. "I must have lost my memory in the fire that destroyed my home, family and all of my friends. Somehow, I escaped, but now, here it is happening all over again, and I must be the one to blame!" Happy, coming to this sudden conclusion, came to a quick stop. He wiped the tears out of his eyes with a droopy little leaf from one of his branches and glanced back at the terrible disaster that was happening to the forest that had befriended him.

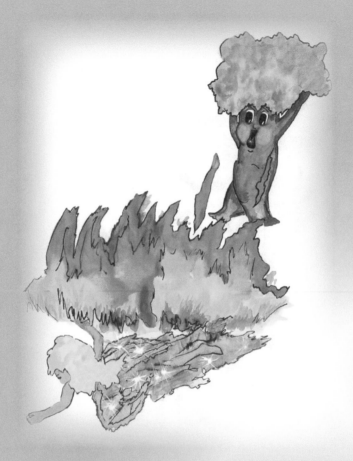

As he was wiping his tears, he saw something and heard a small whimper. "Oh! Someone is in trouble! I must go back and help," he thought as he risked his life to go back into the smoke-filled air. Desperately trying to see through the smoke, he stumbled over some sticks and fell flat on his face again! He blinked, not believing what lay ahead of him. Happy stood up and ran towards the Joy Baby just as the fire caught onto her sparkles. He looked around for some water, but there wasn't any! In desperation, Happy Tree fluffed the fire out with his top knot and brushed away the ashes with his leaves.

He scooped up the frightened little Angie Baby and gently carried her away to the safety of the meadow. The Baby was crying softly as Happy sat on the grass, rocking her gently. The green meadow was filled with the scent of heather and wild flowers, roses and golden broom. They both breathed the fresh air deeply, trying to force the smoke out of their lungs. As they rested, the bald eagle, Enoch, flew overhead. Twig and the other Joy Babies ran up to them. They fanned the smoke away from the Happy Tree. Happy began coughing and sneezing and his bark was still smoking from the heat of the fire.

21

The Joy Babies ran down to the brook and dipped water to rub on his bark so it would cool him. They gave some water to their sister. "Thank you," said the Happy Tree and the Joy baby, "We feel much better now." Everyone looked startled as Blu the Bluebird flew up. He was fluttering all about. "Boy! Are you in trouble!" chirped Blu. "Why?" asked Angie. "Because they think Happy is the one that…" Blu Blubird stopped in mid-air and gasped! With a wing to his mouth, Blu started to giggle! Enoch, the eagle, flew up and over Joyland until he spotted the Joy Baby and the Happy Tree. He was satisfied they were safe so he flew back to tell the Elders.

Meanwhile Blu the Blue Bird pointed at The Happy Tree as Angie looked up at his top knot and started laughing. The Joy Babies, Twig and all the wood creatures stood staring at the little tree. Their eyes were wide with surprise. "What is so funny?" asked Happy. Angie pulled Happy to his feet, still laughing, while Blu tugged at "LOOK!" everyone exclaimed as they all looked in the water. Suddenly the Joy Babies heard the Elders of Joyland calling to them. The Joy Babies told The Happy Tree and Angie Baby they were going back to face the music. "We will be back as soon as we can," said Sharon Baby. Angie Baby told them she was staying with The Happy Tree and she waved goodbye as the Joy Babies flew back to Joyland.

CHAPTER 4

The Discovery

"Come with us and we'll show you!" the others said as they led The Happy Tree back to the Magic Brook. Happy finally understood as he bent down on his trunk and looked in the water to see his reflection. He was not sure whether to believe what he saw. For, you see, when Happy fluffed out the fire to save Angie Baby, the chlorophyll that made his foliage green went out of his leaves, and he had suddenly become quite purple! Angie and Blu were still laughing. He looked at them quite bewildered. "I don't think this is funny at all!" he exclaimed.

"Why, Happy, we're not laughing at you," said the Joy Baby. "At least we don't mean to be laughing. Whoever heard of a purple Happy tree?" exclaimed Blu. The situation had become too much for Happy. He wearily plumped down on the grass and buried his face in his leaves. "Boo, hoo, hoo!" The Morning Glory was shocked to see Happy turn purple right before her eyes.

25

"It's not enough to finally discover my true identity and realize I'm an orphan without a home, and that it's all my fault for causing all this damage to the only friends I have. But now, being purple is just too much! Boo, hoo, hoo!" Blu and Angie Baby stopped laughing. Blu perched on Happy Tree's top knot and bending over, looked him in the eye and said, "We're sorry, Happy. Oh, please don't cry. We don't care if you're purple or green. It's not what's on the outside that counts, it's what is on the inside!"

"That's right," Angie Baby said. "Don't worry. Everything will be all right." But Happy knew everything was not all right. Everything was all wrong and he didn't know how to fix it.

"Well, now what?" Happy asked Blu. Blu replied, "I came to warn you that Mayor Roots has everyone up in limbs because he thinks you are the one that deliberately left all that trash and started the fire. Now he's calling a Tree Town Council Meeting with all the elders. You both are in a lot of trouble!"

Angie started crying. "Oh, no! What about my Joy brother and my Joy sisters? Where are they? Are they okay?"

"I don't know. I was just supposed to find you and tell you to come to the Tree Town Council Meeting," Blu chirped. "No way!" said Happy. "It's time for me to be moving on. I'm going to run away!"

"Oh, no," said Angie Baby, "please, Happy, you can't leave me!"

"Well," Happy said, standing up and brushing the dust from his trunk.

"Why don't you come with me?" He stooped down, encouraging Angie to jump on his top knot. And jump she did! Her little morning glories went limp with her effort, but they spruced up again when she smiled. "Okay! I'm ready! Let's go!" Angie exclaimed gleefully. Blu said he was going to tell Mayor Roots! "Go ahead and tell. Who cares?" replied Angie Baby and Happy. Happy tromped down the hill with Angie Baby holding tightly to his top knot. "One thing about it," Angie said as they ran across the meadow to the bottom of the hill, "at least you are color coordinated!" She was referring to his trunk and limbs becoming a bluish grey when his leaves turned purple. "Yeah? Who cares?" answered the sad little tree. They spotted the pou pou tree but they did not stop. "Hey wait for me," said Frederick Fox. "Me too!" cried Smiley Skunk.

"Oh, come on, please wait for us guys, STOP! We don't wanna miss anything!"

"We are out of here! You will have to catch up!" yelled the little tree to the upset animals.

Happy Tree knew he had done nothing wrong and he was not going to hang around any longer to find out.

"No one tells us anything until the last minute! No wonder I am always late" yelled the POU POU tree!

"That's OK," whispered little doe, "just stay here and take a nap with me."

"I am tired after this fire and that sounds good to me," he replied. "I didn't see you over there! You sure blend in with your surroundings."

With Angie Baby and the Happy Tree gone and with the other Joy Babies going to the Town Council meeting to explain their side of the story, there was no reason not to rest awhile, thought the coconut tree. Well, it was not long before Blue Bluebird was spreading the news all over Joyland! He landed on top of Mikie Baby's head and blurted out the story to the whole Tree Town Council Meeting about Happy Tree and Angie Baby and how they said they were running away!

Mayor Roots turned to the Joy Babies. "Did the Happy Tree start this fire?" "Oh, no, sir," replied Mikie, "it was our fault, not The Happy Tree's!"

"We were putting trash in the barrel and then we were looking at a butterfly and the pretty colors through a magic glass Karen Baby and the Happy Tree had found and the glass started the fire and…"

At that same moment, a very serious discussion was going on. "You had better not let me catch you playing with that strange tree again, Twig!" scolded Wally B. Walnut. "I don't want you to get involved with someone like that. He is nothing but trouble. After all we have done to take care of the Joy Babies!" fussed Ellie Elm to the little children.

32

Sassy Sassafras shook her head, "Who in the world ever heard of a tree turning purple? Just as well that he is gone. He was really weird!"

Mayor Roots does not like to be interrupted!

"Who is calling who weird?" cried the Pou, Pou Tree as he entered the clearing after trying to catch up with his friends, The Happy Tree and Angie baby. "I said, who is calling who weird, Little Lady?" cried the Pou, Pou Tree! "HUH?"

"I look different too!" cried the Pou Pou tree. **"I AM A COCONUT TREE!"** "I wasn't talking about you, so be quiet you crazy tree!" Sassy replied. "I just don't like anyone talking against the Happy Tree, so just remember you are not the only one here in Joyland and a lot of us love Happy Tree. We don't think he is weird either!" answered the little coconut tree.

"Alright everyone quiet!" shouted Mayor Roots. "Do not interrupt me again! As I said it was our fault, not Happy Tree's. We were putting trash in the barrel and then we were looking at a butterfly and the pretty colors through a magic glass that we had found near Timber Lake," whispered Mikie Baby. "The glass started the fire and…"

"**Aaaaaaaaaaahaaaaaaaaaaa!**" Oadie Oak shouted at Mikie.

"Then you DID start the fire?" replied the Oak tree.

"No, I didn't. None of us did! It was an accident," said Mikie. A big tear welled up in the corner of his eye.

"You leave him alone," cried Karen Baby.

"That's right," said Twig. "You should find out the facts first."

"What do you know? You are only children!" snapped Sassy Sassafras.

"Yes!" exclaimed Ellie Elm. "And ill-mannered children at that!"

"It's not ill-mannered to ask for a chance to explain," said Sharon Baby.

"Alright," replies Wally B. Walnut, "I think we should have a vote to determine who is at fault and what the punishment should be."

"No one was at fault," said the Joy Babies. "The Happy Tree is our friend and has done nothing wrong. He saved Angie's life. I think you should forgive him."

And so it went, far into the night. The elders of Joyland were listening to the Joy Babies giving their reasons why Angie and Happy should be forgiven. But hisses and boos and cries of "No! No!" drowned out the speeches before they were finished. But finally Mayor Roots turned and pointed straight at the Joy Babies. "That being the case, little children," began Mayor Roots, "then this Happy Tree won't be in any trouble.

But if he IS GUILTY! HE WILL BE BANNED from Joyland!"

"Let's get out of here and go find them fast!" said Karen baby. "We have to get Angie back. She cannot live in the forest like a tree!"

"You are right," said Mayor Roots. "We will follow the root prints track left in the soft earth." The tiny wood creatures ran ahead to find tracks. They were used to running and the search would not tire them out so easily.

39

CHAPTER 5

The Journey

Up ahead, the Happy Tree ran and ran and ran, until he could not run anymore. "Put me down and I will run with you," said Angie Baby. Happy put the little girl down on the soft grass.

"I think we have run far enough for now," he said. "Let's just walk for a while, until we are rested." They walked across fields and meadows and walked up a high hill. Just over the hill was a Rain Forest. The trees were big, gloomy and frightening. The sun finished the last rays of its lingering good-byes and the moon rose in awful majesty over the silver tree tops as the pair approached the forbidden forest.

As the two walked towards the Rain Forest, the trees turned to look at them. "Who are those strangers?" someone whispered. "Why it's a funny looking purple tree and one of the Joy Babies. I'll bet they're runaways!" "Hmphmph!" an older tree snorted. Happy Tree was stunned at the sound of the mean sounding trees! So, he picked himself up then bent over so Angie could jump up onto his top knot again, and off they ran… away from the trees that were scaring them They ran as hard as they could, past many gnarled and twisted trees, some shaking their limbs in anger. The further they went, the harder it was to tell where they were.

The twisted trees were shaking their limbs in anger.

The further they went, the harder it was to tell where they were. Finally, Happy came to the conclusion that they were lost! Confused Happy walked faster, but he only ended up deeper into the scary woods. "**Donnnn't come in here**!" warned a ghostly voice coming from the darkness. Angie became frightened as she stared up at the speckled tree. "Excuse me," began Angie, and then she stopped, terrified, in the middle of a sentence.

42

The monster tree reached down and lifted Happy up high into the air revealing two enormous looking eyes, frosted like ice.

"Get out of our Rain Forest!" he shouted. "We don't like purple trees or children that fly!" The mean, ugly tree let go of Happy and Happy fell on the ground with a thud! Both the Happy Tree and Angie Baby ran as fast as they could to get away from that tree.

They spent the night in the Rain Forest, snuggling down between the roots of a big, spooky tree. Happy tried to find a comfortable place where the wood did not stick into Angie's wounded wings. The night was warm and the moon was bright. A soft breeze blew across the treetops. Often and with no warning, rain would filter down from the leaves of the eerie trees. Out of nowhere, Thunder appeared to protect them.

The two runaways were surprised to see Thunder. "If we go back, we will get into a lot of trouble," said Happy. Big drops of water fell from the sky. Angie was getting wet and cold. She started to cry. The Happy Tree could not bear to see his friend unhappy and his branches drooped sadly. He picked Angie up and got on Thunder, the horse started running through the Rain Forest.

45

It was getting dark and the trees were making spooky sounds. In a little while, Thunder slowed down and let them get down and rest. The two runaways were wet and sad. Happy Tree's little purple leaves began to droop. Angie became cross. Her sparkles were getting dim because the morning glories had closed in the rain. Her lovely, long curls became damp, and soaking wet. It was still night so they decided to rest under a spooky tree where they would be out of the rain.

Deep into the night, Happy told Angie where he came from. He told her stories about his family being destroyed in a gigantic forest fire. But, along with the bad stories, he told her interesting tales about his adventures on the way to Joyland. He told her about waking up in the river after he got out of the fire and found out he was floating down the river with the Pou Pou Tree, and that is how he had met him. Happy explained the rainforest trees are not that bad. He explained why the rainforest trees and plants are known for breathing in carbon dioxide and they breathe out oxygen. That is what we all need. Trees and plants are very important!

The mean trees are only trying to scare off strangers who might destroy the rain forest but Angie was too tired to listen. She smiled and closed her eyes. The Happy Tree's soft voice finally put the exhausted Joy Baby into a deep sleep. Gently he covered her with leaves so she would not get chilled. When the dew sprinkled down on Angie Baby's morning glories, totally wilted from their exciting adventures, they sleepily rubbed their eyes, fluttering their eyelashes at the frightening trees hovering over them. It wasn't the morning dew. The rain forest trees were angrily shaking their limbs and uttering low, weird sounds causing rain to fall on the runaways.

Spooked, Happy grabbed the wide-eyed child and ran down the winding path bouncing the floppy morning glories all over each other. "Boy! What an experience!" exclaimed Happy, as he ran out of the forest into the brightness of the new day. Angie Baby was tired and hungry. "I want something to eat," she pouted. "I'm thirsty too!" Happy looked around. "Don't worry, I'll find something for you," he said cheerfully. "There are lots of berries for you to eat." But it was raining so hard, it was even hard to find a berry bush. When they did, she hungrily gobbled them up.

49

"Over here," a call came from The Happy Tree. "I've found a Sugar Maple fountain. You may drink all you like." Angie Baby ran to the Sugar Maple but waited for Happy to help her.

"By the way, I am hungry," she said as she ran back to pick more berries in the downpour, "and thirsty."

She began crying as Happy led her back to the Sugar Maple Fountain. Happy pushed a knot in the Maple Tree's trunk and syrup flowed out. Angie gratefully drank all her little tummy could hold. She noticed that Happy Tree did not eat any of the berries or drink from the Sugar Maple Fountain. "Why don't you eat and have something to drink?" asked the curious child. The Happy Tree smiled at the bright- eyed little girl.

"Well," he began, "I don't eat like you do. I get my nourishment from the sun and from the ground. The sun's rays help me grow strong and tall, and the ground gives me my food and water. It goes into my roots and then up into all my leaves and branches to help me grow. So," he continued, "you might say that I eat all the time!" Angie smiled up at him. She was very glad that she had the Happy Tree for a friend, but she was still tired and frightened and wanted to go home. The two were exhausted and were soon asleep. The night went slow.

Just as the sun started to shine bright and the birds were flying about and singing, the two were awakened by the sound of a familiar voice.

"Yooohooo, children," Angie and Happy looked around. There was a big, tree standing in a small clearing by a stream. It was a rather strange looking tree. Angie recognized her as Wilma Willow.

"Oh, are we glad to see you!" said the Joy Baby. "Have you met The Happy Tree?"

53

CHAPTER 6

The Scolding

"Oh, my! He doesn't look very happy to me," said Wilma. She was referring to his pouting face and droopy purple leaves.

"You look a little strange," she commented.

Wilma Willow had decided not to go to the Tree Town Council Meeting. She was too worried about the little missing Joy Baby and wanted to find her. Just then it started to rain again. As she walked towards them, she held her limbs up high, trying to open a dry place for the two of them to come inside.

"Oh, Angie Baby! I'm so glad to see that you're both safe! Please come over here and get out of the rain! You may crawl up under my branches and I'll keep you safe and warm until the rain stops." Happy scooped Angie Baby up into his branches because her poor little broken wings still would not flutter. Wilma became concerned. "Oh, you poor, little Joy Baby, come here and let me doctor you up!" Wilma fussed. She bandaged up Angie Baby's wings with willow leaves and gave her a big kiss. Angie Baby smiled and thanked her.

55

She explained to Wilma how The Happy Tree had saved her. Wilma seemed so relieved. "Oh Happy, you both should go back and face the Town Council. The truth always comes out in the end. Everyone will forgive you. You must face your problems. Never, ever run away from them!" Angie and Happy listened intently as the motherly willow tree preached her advice.

"Maybe I was wrong to leave this way," thought Happy.

"I guess I should at least take Angie Baby back to her friends and family," he finally said aloud. "But I can't go back, now that I'm purple, everyone thinks I'm weird and nobody wants anything to do with me. They would not listen before. Why would they listen now?" said the sad little tree. "I can certainly see why you would be upset," said Wilma. "But, running away is not the way to solve your problems." "We know that now," said the little tree, as he hung his top branches downward.

The sun was shining brightly, and the birds were singing. Flowers perked up their petals, and bugs, bees, and butterflies were flying all about. Happy and Angie looked back at the edge of the Rain Forest. Scary trees swaying and moaning. Angie Baby was glad to be leaving the scary place. "We're going back to Joyland," Happy told his friends. "I think you have made a very wise decision Happy!" said Wilma Willow. "Thank you," replied Happy. "And if we're ever in this meadow again, we will stop to visit you." "I visit Joyland quite often to gossip with all of my friends," said Wilma. While they were talking, Angie's attention had been diverted.

"LOOK OVER THERE!" shouted Angie. Everyone was startled at the little Joy Baby's excitement.

CHAPTER 7

The Gold Dwarf

ARAINBOW!

"LOOK OVER THERE!" shouted Angie. Everyone was startled at the little Joy Baby's excitement. It was a beautiful rainbow, just like the one in the magnifying glass. "What makes a rainbow, Happy?" asked one of the wood creatures. "The sun makes it when the colors of the sun shines through the raindrops," replied the Happy Tree. "Look, I see the end of it!" called out the Happy Tree, as he ran toward the spot where the colors ended.

"Come back!" Wilma Willow cried out. "You promised me you were going to go home!"

"We will," shouted Happy, "but not until we touch the rainbow!" The others scurried after the little tree, not sure why they wanted to find the end of the rainbow. Wilma Willow just stood there and lowered her branches in disappointment.

"I guess they didn't know there's a rainbow after it rains," she thought to herself.

Finally, they all came to the edge of a small valley where the colors fell into a big black pot. There on the ground was a strange looking character wearing funny clothing and an odd shaped hat. The wood creatures backed up when they saw the strange man looking in their direction. But not the Happy Tree! All his life he had wanted to see what happened at the end of a rainbow, and now, this was his big chance. The little man was dragging a sack toward the big pot as the Happy Tree and Angie Baby neared him.

61

"Who are you?" asked Happy, "and what are you doing with that big black pot?"

"I'm the Gold Dwarf," replied the little man, "and I put gold in the pot."

"But where does the gold come from, Gold Dwarf?" asked Angie Baby.

"I make it," replied the Dwarf. "I pound the sun's rays on my magic anvil and make these large, gold coins. I store them in my polka-dotted sack until a rainbow appears and then I fill up the pot." The Gold Dwarf looked suspiciously at the little tree and the small child.

"You didn't come here to steal my gold, did you?" inquired the little man, "because if you did, you won't get away with it. Someone keeps taking my gold. I haven't figured out who it is yet, but I'll catch him!"

The Gold Dwarf eyed the strange purple tree and the human child with wings and became even more suspicious. He had never seen anything quite like them before.

"Oh, no!" cried Happy. "We would never steal your gold. We just wanted to know what was here.

My name is the Happy Tree. And this is my friend, Angie Baby."

"The little girl looks normal, except for the wings," said the Gold Dwarf. "But **Whoever heard of a purple tree**?" A little hurt by the Gold Dwarf's remark, Happy decided not to let it interfere with his decision to find out everything he could about the rainbow. "Mr. Gold Dwarf, may I please touch the end of the rainbow? I promise, I won't hurt it," begged Happy Tree. The little man stared at the tree for a few minutes and then replied.

"I don't see why not, I don't know why it would hurt anything," answered the little man, "but I don't think you can reach that far, and the pot is too high for you to climb."

They thought and thought but could not figure a way to get to the top of the pot. The Gold Dwarf suggested, "Angie why don't you fly to the top?" "I'm afraid to. You see, my wings were injured in a fall and they are still bandaged. I don't think they're quite strong enough, yet! Even if they were, I am too small to carry Happy Tree."

"Well, then," decided the Gold Dwarf, "I'll build some stairs with the gold coins and you can climb up to the top."

"That's brilliant!" shouted Happy Tree to the Gold Dwarf.

"Yes, it is," said the dwarf as he shined his fingernails on his vest. So, the Gold Dwarf, Happy Tree and Angie Baby busied themselves with the chore of building the stairs. Finally, he reached down to help up Angie Baby. Suddenly, one of Happy's roots got caught in the green ray of the rainbow, and it began to lift him up into the sky. Happy held onto Angie's hand tightly as they were pulled up with a vacuum force into the ray of the rainbow.

The Gold Dwarf looked up and shook his fist. "**Now, you've done it**!" he shouted. "Come down this instant before you really get into trouble!" But the mischievous pair could not come down. In fact, they did not even hear the Gold Dwarf because they were caught in the rainbow and were going higher and higher! They tumbled over and over as if they were in a long, green tunnel. Playful starbursts of color danced merrily about them as they tumbled and rolled with the vacuum that had them trapped. They were so busy having fun that they did not realize the danger ahead.

CHAPTER 8

The Green Ray

Soon they were at the top of the rainbow. The Happy Tree and Angie Baby looked down and could see the Gold Dwarf far below them, standing next to his big black pot. At the edge of the little valley, they could see the tiny wood creatures who were still afraid to go near the little man. Further, still, they could see the Sugar Maple Fountain, the stream, and Wilma Willow. Far in the distance was Joyland, where they could just make out Twig, Lara LaQuack, Sassy Sassafras, Fum Ming and his wife, Ching, and other folks from Joyland.

The colors were brilliant! Pinks, soft blues and soft hues. Stars and sparkles were everywhere. Angie's morning glories were having a great time laughing and trying to stay entwined in her golden locks as they were tossed about. One fell out, but Happy caught it and playfully tucked it into his purple foliage. The yards and yards of glimmery sparkles wrapped around Angie and were floating all about her. They were getting tangled in her silver wings. The bandages worked their way off, and she fluttered her wings to see if they were all right. They were! She could fly again!

She fluttered them and flew to the edge of the green ray. She could touch the pink ray and the yellow ray, but she could not go inside them. It was as if she was flying up against a glass wall. She was so happy that her wings were working again! The face of the sun was hidden by the rainbow as Blu Bluebird flitted about chirping and pecking wildly at the green ray. The beautiful valley and surrounding hills echoed with his singing. Angie Baby and Happy Tree tried to wave and thank Blu, but they found themselves falling and diving past the stars.

CHAPTER 9
Frederick Fox

Suddenly, they had begun to slide down the other side of the rainbow. Faster and faster they went until it almost took their breath away. Going up the rainbow was great fun but going down was another story altogether. They fell past the sun and even the moon. They mingled with the birds and with raindrops which fell in a sudden cool shower. The colors were glistening and bouncing off the walls of the long green tunnel. They went whizzing and zooming out of control.

They slipped and slid holding on to each other, continuing to skid faster and faster, down towards the earth. They saw fields and the meadow, Joyland and the Rain Forest and finally the end of the rainbow. Their friends were standing in and staring into rain puddles where everything was reflected in an upside down world! As they got near the end, they could see where the rainbow was coming from.

At the end of the rainbow, stirring big pots of dye, was a sly, stern looking fox. For each color in the rainbow, the fox had a pot of dye that he had mixed. A big, black pot just like the one the Gold Dwarf used. As Happy Tree and Angie Baby neared the end, the fox saw them, jumped off his ladder, out of the way of the tumbling pair. Angie sailed over the pot and landed on the side of the hill! But the Happy Tree wasn't so lucky! He came sliding in head first, right into the big pot splashing green dye all over the place.

Angie Baby looked up and noticed the green ray had faded from the beautiful rainbow. Happy Tree pulled himself up to the rim of the pot, green dye dripping from his branches.

"I say," said the fox, "do you realize what you have just done?"

"No sir!" replied Happy as green dye dripped from his branches. "Who are you?"

"I, dear boy, am Frederick Fox, the British Rainbow Dyemaker! And you have just splashed away THE GREEN RAY OF THE RAINBOW!" The Happy Tree peered over the edge of the green dye pot to see Mayor Roots with his branches folded across his trunk.

The little tree climbed out of the pot and tried to shake off the green dye of the rainbow. Behind Mayor Roots stood Joyland, the wood creatures, his friend Twig, and the other Joy Babies. The Happy Tree was certain everyone was very angry with him. But, to his surprise, he was greeted with joy. Oh, the laughter and song that resounded through the land! Oh, how the bells rang, the birds chirped, and the trees shook their branches when Happy bent down to look in the puddle of water left by the rain and saw his foliage was green again!

CHAPTER 10
Joyland Forgives

The Happy Tree was green again! It was true. The dye had made his leaves green again. Happy Tree danced to think that he wasn't purple anymore! "Now, you look like a real Happy Tree!" laughed Angie. Then, the little Tree's branches dropped in despair. "I may be green again, but everyone still thinks I started the fire in Joyland!" "Not anymore," boomed Mayor Roots in his loud, but friendly voice. "Sometimes," said Wally B. Walnut, "we just don't give you, young children, the benefit of the doubt. Twig and the others told us what actually happened, and what a risk you took, by putting out the fire!"

"There was no way, you could have known that the magnifying glass was dangerous," chimed in Ellie Elm, "but, even though it wasn't your fault, what is important is that we have all learned from this experience. You should have stayed and told your side of the story, too, Happy."

"I know that now," said Happy Tree, "and if you let me come back to Joyland, I promise I will try to be more responsible."

"We have neglected you in the past because you were not like some of the rest of us," said Sassy Sassafrass, "but, we will try to make it up to you." "If you like," added Fu Ming, "you may stay with me and Mrs. Ming. We were different when we first came to Joyland, just like you.But now we are part of everything. We do not have any little trees of our own and we would be glad to have you live with us. You can come back and stay this time, Happy," said Twig, "and the Joy Babies can visit any time." "Not only that, but you will be the official Happy Tree of Joyland," said Oadie Oak. The Happy Tree could not have been happier. "Thank you all very much," he said. "I will be more careful in the future."

CHAPTER 11
Going Home

It had been a long day for everyone. The final rays of the sun's light were resting on the hilltops. The air was growing dark with the coming of dusk and the last sunbeam left the hills. The Joy Babies sparkles began to dim as the whole group started toward Joyland together. On the way, they stopped to say good-bye to Wilma Willow. The Joy Babies drank from the Sugar Maple Fountain, and the wood creatures drank from the stream, while Lara LaQuack bathed her Quacklings.

They had not traveled far when they met an old man hobbling wearily towards the castle. He appeared tired from a long journey. He limped along the roadway. He had a big round belly and his head was almost bald. He had a large sack on his back, and when approached and questioned by the children about what was in his sack, the strange looking man yelled, "That's none of your business!" He snapped his fingers, blinked and disappeared! **Poof!** Just then the pou pou tree rounded the corner just as the man disappeared! "Where did he go this time? He keeps disappearing, I followed him from Gold Dwarf's pots of gold, talk about someone weird! When the Gold Dwarf came back, he disappeared!"

Mikie Baby looked at the other Joy Babies in wonderment and said, "Do you suppose that's the man who's been stealing from the Gold Dwarf?" A nearby toad croaked, "That was Rainbosak! You'll have a hard time catching him or proving that he is the one stealing the gold!" Mayor Roots quickly shushed everyone and told them to mind their own business. He felt the Joy Babies and The Happy Tree had enough excitement for the time being. The mystery of the vanishing gold coins would just have to wait for another day. As they walked past the other trees in the neighboring Rain Forest, the Happy Tree and the others said good-bye. The Rain Forest trees shook their branches at them warning, "**Don't come back**." **No problem**! That was the last place Happy and Angie ever wanted to visit again!

On the way back home, the Joy babies flew and flitted and played with the wood creatures, Twig and the Happy Tree. As the Sun was hanging lazily in the western sky, his rays made an orange color across the beautiful, green meadow. The Happy Tree and the Joy Babies laughed and playfully dancing into their next exciting adventure in Joyland.

The End...

Happy was so happy that he felt like he was on top of the world!

ABOUT THE AUTHOR

Joyce Timberlake

thepurplehappytree@gmail.com

Author, Artist

Happy **T**ree books, lyrics for poems and songs, videos, and related products, lecturing, storytelling and demonstrating the art techniques she used in the books is part of Ms. Timberlakes' agenda. Educating children about the reforestation project and the importance of trees is the main slant of her lectures and demonstrations. She has traveled nationwide for years attending trade shows, art shows and festivals promoting and selling HAPPY TREE products for infants, toddlers, teens and adults.

The national theme is **"Everybody should have a HAPPY TREE"** by Joy. Joyce Timberlake has been featured in several national publications and was selected as one of the nations' leading artists to be represented in **"The International Society of Female Professionals,"** a National Women's organization in New York. Ms. Timberlake was also featured in an article in May 2021 in the **Pretty Women Hustle magazine** published in London, England with a circulation of 500,000 homes and social media. She is also a member of **Marquis Who's Who** in New York.

Below are organizations which Ms. Timberlake has been recognized in through the years:

Covington's Who's Who

Who's in American Art

Artists' USA (Several Years)

Women Artist in America

American Printmakers

13th International Annual Book

Altogether there are many ideas for books and lyrics for songs. Joyce Timberlake conceived the idea for the "HAPPY TREE" in 1964, when her "Joy Babies" were toddlers. Being an artist and a writer, she remembered thinking, "Oh, that's so cute!" when she drew a tree skipping down a hill holding hands with two children. She immediately drew a happy little face on the tree, and the HAPPY TREE was born. Joyce Timberlake is a nationally known wildlife artist and has been involved in conservation programs for over 20 years. She has had three television series on art, published art magazines, and served as art critic for several newspapers. She has owned and operated several art galleries and schools and has taught as many as eight different subjects in 12 different classes per week. She began teaching art in 1965 out of her home studio which eventually led her to open her own art school, The Timberlake Art Academy.

The Editor

Angelcia Carol Wright

Writer, Photographer & Songwriter.

The following lyrics for songs were written by Ms. Wright and archived for the Happy Tree Series;

The Happy Tree
Song Of The Rainbow
Take Time for the Children, and many more.

Angelcia has won many awards for her photography and her writings.

Among her current list of books written and published:

Ghost Ships Of The James River
Whispering Wings, My walk with God
Candy, My dog.
Orbs, What are they?
Visions Or Dreams

The Happy Tree's SMART CORNER

The Happy Tree is just like you and me. He laughs, he dances and he has fun. Once in a while his brain kicks in. He calls this his "Brain Storm." When this happens, he will have an answer for almost any question you could possibly ask him.

Question: Why does it look like it's raining frogs?

Happy says, "When the sun shines bright, it pulls up the water from the lakes and puddles. The water turns to vapor and the water forms clouds in the sky. But tadpoles live in the water and some of them end up in the tops of trees and even the clouds. The tadpoles grow up to be frogs, so when the water drops stick to each other and gets heavy, it rains and it falls back down into the lakes and puddles. It may wash them out of trees, it may of the clouds and then it looks like it's raining frogs, because it is raining frogs!"

CPSIA information can be obtained
at www.ICGtesting.com
Printed in the USA
BVHW052105211121
622102BV00002B/9